black-eyed susan

Sophie loved flowers...

harebell

The author would like to thank the many writers and readers who lent an eye and an ear to these stories on their way to final draft, including Sue Bristol, Pat Gedbaw, Annette Markin, Nancy Moreland, Cheryl Paden, Jean Patrick, Leslie Shanahan, Janet Todd, Karla Wendelin, Joyce Winfield, and the members of the Metro Novelists. I can never thank you enough!

Published by Prairieland Press
PO Box 2404
Fremont, NE 68026-2404
Printed in U.S.A.

www.bangprinting.com
Code 293471
Bang Printing Brainerd MN

Book design by Lynn Gibney
The text of this book is set in 15-point Baskerville.

10 9 8 7 6 5 4 3 2 1
First Edition

Library of Congress Cataloging-in-Publication data
Sharp, N.L.
The flower girl ; The ring bear / N.L. Sharp ; illustrated by Timothy James Hantula.
p. cm.
SUMMARY: Created in flip-over format, this book details the experiences of two children preparing to be the flower girl and ring bearer in an upcoming wedding.
Audience: Ages 0-9.   LCCN: 2009930967
ISBN-10: 0-975-98293-1   ISBN-13: 978-0-975-98293-8

[1. Weddings—Fiction. 2. Flower girls—Fiction. 3. Ring bearers—Fiction.
4. Aunts—Fiction. 5. Uncles—Fiction.] I. Hantula, Timothy James. II. Title.
[E]—dc22
PZ7.S5316 Fl 2010   2009930967

The Flower Girl

by

N.L. Sharp

illustrated by

Timothy James Hantula

Sophie *loved* flowers. She loved real flowers and fake flowers and flowers in fields. She loved pink flowers and purple flowers and yellow flowers. She even loved to eat flowers. Candy flowers and cookie flowers and cauliflowers. So she wasn't surprised when her mom said she was going to be the flower girl in her Uncle Dan's wedding.

"What does a flower girl do?" Sophie asked.

"You walk down the aisle, carrying a basket of rose petals," Mom said.

"What happens if I drop it?" Once, she was carrying a bowl of water for her cat, Max. It tipped, and water splashed all over the laundry room floor.

"Don't worry," Mom said. "You're supposed to drop the petals. That way, the bride will have a path to follow as she walks down the aisle."

"Do I have to wear a flower costume?" Sophie asked.

"No. You'll wear a dress," Mom said. "A sparkly white dress with lace and beads and flowers in your hair."

Sophie smiled. I'll look
just like a princess, she thought.
This was going to be fun!

Sophie wanted to be the best flower girl she could, so she practiced every day. She curtsied to her mom. She danced with her dad. And she marched around the garden with a bowl of cereal, sprinkling it on the grass so Max would have a path to follow.

Finally, there was only one day left before the wedding.
"Sophie, it's time to go to the church," Dad said.

"Why are we going there?" Sophie asked.

"We're going to practice our parts for the wedding,
so tomorrow we'll know just what to do."

"I've been practicing," Sophie said. "Every day."

"Good," Dad said. "I'm proud of you. But tonight,
Uncle Dan wants everyone to practice together."

Sophie looked at her clothes. "Where's my dress?" she asked.

"Here it is."
Mom took a box
out of the closet.

She helped Sophie slip the dress
over her head.

Sophie stared at herself in the mirror.
"Do I really get to wear this?" she asked.

"Yes," Mom said.

"Where's my crown?" Sophie asked.

"Here." Mom placed
a wreath of flowers on her head.

Sophie twirled around
in front of the mirror.

"Look at me," Sophie said.
"I'm a princess. A beautiful flower princess."

"Take it off," Mom said.
"We don't want to get it dirty before tomorrow."
She hung the dress back in the closet.

Soon it was time to go. Sophie was so excited, she could hardly sit still while they drove
down the street. And when Dad stopped the car, Sophie couldn't believe her eyes. The church
looked just like a castle!

There was a boy standing in front of the church. "This is Robert," Mom said.
"You're going to walk down the aisle with him."

"Are you my prince?" Sophie asked.

"I'm no prince!" said Robert. "I'm the ring bear."

"A bear?"

Sophie asked. "I have to walk
down the aisle with a bear?"
"Yes," said Dad. "Didn't you know?"

"No!" said Sophie. "How can I be a princess if I'm walking with a bear?"

"You're not going to be a princess," Dad said. "You're going to be the flower girl."

Sophie shook her head. **"NO!"** she said. "I won't. I want to be a princess. If I can't be a princess, I'm not going to be in the wedding!"

"You have to be in the wedding," Mom said. "Uncle Dan is counting on you."

"Someone else can drop the petals," Sophie said.

"I don't want someone else," Uncle Dan said. "I want you."

Sophie sat down on the curb. She thought about
how much fun it had been practicing to be a princess.
Then she thought about how sad Uncle Dan looked when
she said she wasn't going to be in his wedding.

"Is it true you need someone to make a path
for the bride to follow?" she asked.

"Yes, Sophie, it is,"
Uncle Dan said.
"And do you really want me
to be the one to do it?"
"Yes," he said. "It wouldn't
be the same without you."
Sophie curtsied. "All right,"
she said. "I'll do it."

The next day, Sophie wore
her long white dress
with a wreath of flowers
in her hair.

She walked down the aisle dropping petals
for the bride to follow. And everyone agreed,
she was the ***best flower girl*** they had ever seen.

Later, at the reception, she curtsied to her mom. She danced with her dad. And she marched around the tables with a bowl of confetti, sprinkling it on the floor so that Robert, her ring bear prince, would have a path to follow.

And everyone agreed, she was the
best flower princess
they had ever seen, too.

And everyone agreed, he was the

best ring bear

they had ever seen, too.

He ate berries
(which were really mints)
and drank honey
(which was really punch).

And he crawled around with his pillow
on his back, trying to keep the ring pop
(which his new Uncle Dan had given him)
from falling on the floor.

Later, at the reception,
he growled at the flower girl.

The next day, Robert wore
his black suit with its long tail, white shirt
and red bow tie. He carried the pillow
down the aisle and held the rings until
the minister wanted them. And everyone
agreed, he was the **best ring bearer**
they had ever seen.

"Yes, Robert, it is," Aunt Jane said.
"And do you really want me to be the one to carry them?"
"Yes, I do. It wouldn't be the same without you."
Robert growled. "All right,"
he said. "I'll do it."

Robert sat down on the curb. He thought about
how much fun it had been practicing to be a bear.
Then he thought about how sad Aunt Jane looked
when he said he wasn't going to be in her wedding.

"Is it true you can't get married
without those rings?" he asked.

"No!" said Robert. "How can I be a bear
when the wedding is in a church?"
"You're not going to be a bear," Mom said.
"You're going to be a ring bearer."
"You mean I don't get to wear a bear suit
and growl and carry the pillow on my back?"
"No, that would be silly. People don't
have bears in their weddings. They have
ring bearers."
Robert stomped his foot. "NO!" he said.
"I want to be a bear. If I can't be a bear,
I'm not going to be in the wedding!"
"You have to be in the wedding," Dad said.
"Aunt Jane needs you. She can't get married
without those rings."
"Someone else can carry them,"
Robert said.
"I don't want someone else,"
Aunt Jane said. "I want you."

But the car did not go to any of those places.
Instead, his dad drove straight to a church.
"What are we doing here?" Robert asked.
"Is this where the wedding will be?"
"Yes," said Mom. "Didn't you know?"

Soon it was time to go. Robert wondered
where the wedding would be. Would it be
in his grandmother's back yard? Maybe it was
in a park or at the zoo!

"Are you sure this is what
I'm supposed to wear?" he asked.
"Yes," Mom said.
"Where's the tail?"
Mom pointed to a long flap
on the back of the jacket.

Robert looked at the flap. Then he looked
at his bears. Maybe I'm supposed to be
a dancing bear, he thought, like in the circus.
"Take it off," Mom said. "We don't want
to get it dirty before tomorrow." She hung
the suit back in the closet.

Robert stared at himself in the mirror.
The black suit did not look like a bear suit
to Robert. Instead, it looked like
something his dad wore when he went
to a fancy party.

Finally there was only one day left
before the wedding.

"Robert, it's time for the rehearsal," Dad said.

"Rehearsal? What's that?"

"The rehearsal is like a play. We're going
to practice our parts for the wedding, so tomorrow
we'll know just what to do."

"I've been practicing," Robert said. "Every day."

"Good," Dad said. "I'm proud of you. But tonight
Aunt Jane wants everyone to practice together."

Robert looked at his clothes. "Where's my suit?"
he asked.

"Here it is." Mom took a bag out of the closet.

"Let's try it on," she said. "We want to make sure
that everything fits just right."

Robert wanted to be the best ring bear he could, so he practiced every day.
He growled at the dog. He ate berries (which were really grapes) and drank honey
(which was really apple juice). And he crawled around the house with a pillow
on his back, trying to keep his glow-in-the-dark ring from falling on the floor.

"What does a ring bear do?" Robert asked.

"You carry the pillow that holds the rings," Mom said.

"What happens if I drop it?" Once, he was carrying his plate to the sink. It dropped, and peas rolled all over the kitchen floor.

"Don't worry," Mom said. "The rings will be tied on tight. Even if you drop the pillow, you won't lose the rings."

"What does a ring bear wear?" Robert asked.

"A suit," Mom said. "A black suit with a tail, a white shirt, and a red bow tie."

Robert smiled. I'll look just like a panda bear, he thought. This was going to be fun!

Robert **loved** bears. He loved real bears and stuffed bears and bears in books. He loved black bears and brown bears and polar bears. He even loved to eat bears. Graham cracker bears and cinnamon bears and chocolate bears. So he wasn't surprised when his mom said he was going to be the ring bear in his Aunt Jane's wedding.

The Ring Bear

by

N.L. Sharp

illustrated by

Timothy James Hantula

For Larry, my ring bear prince, and all of our cubs.

—*N.L. Sharp*

sloth bear

Robert loved bears...

black
bear